STO

FRIEND OF ACPL

W9-DIT-924

BENKEI THE BOY-GIANT

BENKEI THE BOY-GIANT

Marjorie G. Fribourg
Illustrated by Irv Docktor

STERLING

© Copyright, 1958,
by Sterling Publishing Co., Inc.
121 East 24th Street, New York 10
All rights reserved
Manufactured in the United States of America
Library of Congress Catalog Card No. 58-7609

Foreword

The giant Benkei is remembered all over Japan. For 800 years people have been telling of his strength and courage. So many stories have been told about Benkei that he has become a legend. Japanese campers sing about him around campfires. Mothers and fathers tell tales of this wonderful hero to the young.

But Benkei did not start life as a hero. He had a stormy, difficult and adventurous growing-up. And that is the tale you are about to read. I have, of course, adapted it for the purpose of this book.

CO. SCHOOLS

C440141

The rice bowls scattered all over the floor.

A Strange Child

Hundreds of years ago in the little town of Funada, Japan, a very unusual baby was born.

His name was to be Benkei, and his mother's name was O'Hei.

"Look," said O'Hei to her own father, "my baby has hair down to his waist, and he was born with his teeth already in his mouth."

"How very strange," said her father. "What a surprising grandson I have."

But Benkei's grandfather didn't really know how surprising Benkei was to be. When he was six years old, he was twice as big as other boys his age. By the time he was eight years old, he was a real giant.

Benkei liked being a giant. He liked it when his friend, Gensakie, told him, "Benkei, you run as fast as the wind." He liked to see the older boys marvel when he climbed the highest trees or scrambled up the steepest mountain cliff. It was no trouble at all for Benkei. And Benkei liked it especially when Gensakie told him, "Nobody will ever beat you in a fight, Benkei. You're the biggest and the strongest boy in the village."

Of course, being so big for his age, Benkei was very

awkward and always in trouble. One evening in his family's little hut, he knocked down the large, painted screen and overturned the tiny table. The rice bowls scattered all over the floor.

His grandfather was most annoyed. "Cho, cho," he screamed, pulling one hand out of his kimono sleeve and shaking it furiously.

"Worthless, stupid, useless boy," he shouted at poor Benkei, who really couldn't help what he had done.

Benkei darted out of the house and went hurrying up the mountainside. There he was out of harm's way. From the top of a tall fir tree he could just glimpse the sea. Benkei settled down in the branches to watch the rippling water and to think.

"I wish I were a knight in handsome armor," he thought. "I'd love to belong to some royal household. I'd love to be a knight for the wonderful young Prince Yoshitsune. Everyone loves him. I'd like to be part of his household. But more than anything, I wish I weren't always in trouble," he thought as he watched the sun sinking fast behind the mountain.

At last it was quite dark and Benkei picked his way down the snow-capped slopes toward home. His wooden clogs crunched on the frosty path. The wind whistled through his coarse, homespun, kimono-like shirt and flimsy pants. Even his thick underclothes could not keep out the cold.

8

*From the top of a
tall fir tree
he could just
glimpse the sea.*

He was glad to get home. But when he reached the hut, his troubles had only begun.

O'Hei had lit the gay paper lantern. She had fixed the family a wonderful supper. Their bowls were filled with fish, barley, dumplings and radishes. But her face was very stern. Benkei's grandfather looked angry too.

"Benkei, I'm tired of your stupid idleness," he scolded, holding his chopsticks above his bowl. "I'm tired of your getting into mischief. Tomorrow you will start work helping me in my iron shop. You can help mend pots and knives and learn to do other things."

"Honorable Grandfather, the other boys still play around the village. They do not have to work," Benkei complained.

"They are not as big as you," his grandfather said.

"And they do not eat as much," said O'Hei. "With your father gone I have to take in washing. I grow barley. I do all I can. All you do is eat."

Benkei did not like being called stupid and useless. "I'll show them," he murmured, as he stretched out on his sleeping mat. "Anyway, I'm stronger than anybody else."

The next day Benkei followed his grandfather to the iron shop. In the corner was a large hammer. It was so big that no other boy Benkei's age could possibly lift it off the floor. Benkei flung it lazily over his shoulder and held it there with ease.

10

"Wait a minute with that," his grandfather ordered. "I have to heat this metal bar in the fire." The old man held the metal over the flame until it grew red hot. Then he placed the glowing bar on the anvil. "Now hammer," he told Benkei.

"I'll show him," Benkei thought and brought the hammer down on the anvil with all his might.

The building shook. The old man tumbled down. The anvil and the metal bar were driven two feet into the ground.

"Cho! Cho! You idiot! That's not the way to use your strength," screamed the grandfather, as Benkei helped him to his feet. "Now what will I do with you? Go gather firewood since you can do nothing better."

Obediently Benkei left the shop and went off in search of wood. "This time I'll show him," he thought. "This time I'll really show him."

Several of the neighbors were gathering their firewood just outside the village. They called to Benkei, but he did not hear them. He walked right past the low clumps of cherry trees.

"They're not what I want," he thought.

He marched straight past the thick groves of plum trees, and he shook his head. He even tramped past the mighty cedars.

Up, up into the mountains he climbed. He kept going until he came to the biggest pine tree he had ever seen.

It was so tall that it was twice the height of any tree nearby.

"Here it is," Benkei said. "I'll show them." He pulled the huge pine up by the roots. With his bare hands, he pulled it straight up out of the ground.

Carrying the pine on his back, he staggered down the mountain over the slippery rocks. He worked his way along the narrow, crooked path that led to the family hut.

Benkei started to stagger right through the doorway, tree and all.

"Stop," his mother shouted. "Don't bring that in here. Have you no sense?"

Benkei put the tree down. He placed it neatly across the narrow path in front of the hut. Now no one could use the path. The neighbors could not get up over the tree to reach their own homes. It was too big. Soon a crowd gathered in front of the hut.

"Move that tree," they shouted. "We can't get past," they called. They made such a clatter that Benkei's grandfather came running out of his shop to see what was wrong.

"Benkei, what are you doing with that tree?" he demanded.

"It's firewood," Benkei answered.

"Chop it up," shouted his grandfather.

So Benkei got himself a hatchet and went to work. He struck the tree so hard and so fast that the pieces flew in all directions. In no time there was a large spray of wood chips whirling and swirling across the path.

The people were frightened. "Someone may be hurt by that flying wood," a woman said. But Benkei did not listen. At last the neighbors took the hatchet away from Benkei and finished the chopping themselves.

A Strange Temple

Most of the time Benkei just wandered around the mountains chasing the rabbits, the otters and the wild deer.

Sometimes he would just sit near a small pond and listen to the chimes of the beautiful bell of Miidera. Its wonderful music delighted him. The bell seemed to be talking to Benkei and telling him things. More than anything else he loved to hear its loud, clear notes ringing out over the hills until they reached him where he sat. It made him feel happy when he was sad. It calmed him when he was angry.

One day Benkei thought the bell was saying, "Go further up the mountain! Go further up the mountain!" Right away Benkei climbed up over the high cliff, higher up the mountain than he had ever been before. He wandered around until he came to a strange Buddhist temple.

High above the temple was a huge rock. It was at least as big as the temple itself. Benkei could see that this mighty mass of stone was slowly coming loose from the side of the slope. It looked to Benkei as if it was just about to fall upon the temple and crush it to splinters.

"I'd better tell the priests about that rock," he thought.

There was a large brass gate in front of the temple

18

and Benkei pushed it open. Then he walked through a group of cedar trees up to the handsome building, which was painted a bright red.

Inside the priests were at prayer in front of a majestic statue of Buddha. The surrounding cedars outside shut out most of the light and kept the hall dark and mysterious.

Benkei looked around. He had never seen any place to equal the beauty of this temple. The walls were of a fine grained wood. Handsome statues and silver lanterns and brightly colored scrolls caught his eye. The smell of sweet-smelling incense filled the air.

For a few minutes the young Giant stood still in awe and wonder. When he tried to listen to the prayers, he could not understand them. But at last there was a pause in the chanting.

"That rock might fall on you, but I'll move it," Benkei called out over the backs of the praying priests.

Everybody turned around. When they saw a young boy standing behind them, they all smiled.

"You can't move that," a young priest told Benkei.

"Five men couldn't move that," said an elderly Buddhist.

"I'll show you," Benkei shouted.

Benkei scampered up the hillside toward the tremendous rock. At first he could not grip it. He dug his fingers into the soft moss at the edge of the rock until he found a rough place where he could hold on. Then he pulled and jerked and strained. His face grew red. His arms and

21

"Your strength
is no good
unless you use it
wisely,"
said the senior priest.

legs grew stiff. The minutes slid by. The priests began to wander away.

"Leave it alone," they said gently. "You can't move it."

Then slowly the mighty rock came up into Benkei's arms. With all his might Benkei flung it aside. It tumbled over the cliff. Then it went thundering down the mountain-side, crashing down the trees and bushes in its path. For a few minutes the noise was deafening.

The priests were shocked. "Where will that rock land?" they asked each other in wide-eyed horror.

"It will surely destroy whatever it hits," said the senior priest. "What a dreadful thing to do!"

"I'll find out if it's hurt anyone," said the youngest Buddhist priest and hurried away down the mountainside.

Benkei was very hurt. His eyes filled with tears. He had wanted the priests to tell him how wonderful he was.

"Your strength is no good unless you use it wisely," said the senior priest. "Now you had better stay here till we find out what damage that rock has done." He made Benkei sit down under a cherry tree to wait. "Who are you, and what brings you here?" he asked the boy.

"I am Benkei and I often wander around these moun-tains," came the answer.

"Is that all you do?" asked the priest. Benkei nodded. The senior priest shook his head. He was not pleased.

It was almost nightfall when the young Buddhist returned.

"No one has been hurt," he reported. "Some trees have been knocked down, that is all. And the rock has fallen into the sea."

"You are lucky," said the senior priest to Benkei who was still sitting miserably under the cherry tree. "But another time you may not be so fortunate."

Benkei, too, felt grateful that the rock had not hurt anyone.

"Now you must change your useless way of living," the senior priest continued. "I know a merchant in the city. He will take you in and teach you to be useful. We will speak to your family about this."

At first Benkei was not sure he wanted to go. "The mountains are my home," he thought. Still, he did not want to refuse the senior priest.

As he travelled back to the little hut, he wondered what the city might be like. Then the beautiful bell spoke to him again.

"Go to the city, Benkei. Go with the priest," it seemed to say. And Benkei's family was eager for him to go.

At last Benkei decided it might be fun.

Away in the City

Seven days later Benkei followed the senior priest to the city.

The merchant was very busy. All his men were very busy hauling heavy bags of rice. The rice had just been purchased and had to be stacked inside a warehouse. The sky was black and storm clouds were gathering fast. The merchant was afraid that the work could not be finished before the storm. The rice would be spoiled. He was driving his men as hard as they could work and had no time for a useless boy.

Benkei did not like the merchant. He did not like the senior priest. But he felt sorry for the tired workmen. So he gathered up lots of rice bags and tossed them rapidly into the warehouse. He did it all so fast that hours and hours of work were finished in a few minutes.

"Fine! Fine! Well done!" shouted all the men.

The merchant was pleased too. Benkei was delighted. "Well done" was something Benkei didn't hear often. He thought he was going to like the city. He might even like being useful.

"Anyway, I'm stronger than anyone," he thought. "None of these men will ever dare fight with me. I'm sure of that."

The delicate little
paper and wood
house
trembled.

The senior priest had arranged for Benkei to live in the same house with the merchant and his daughter, O'Kin.

O'Kin did not scold Benkei as his family had done. But she thought little of him, and she let him know it. She made Benkei very uncomfortable.

"He eats like an ox," she told her father. "He is a wild, rough country boy, and I do not like him."

Sometimes Benkei could hear her saying these things. But he couldn't think of an answer.

For indeed the merchant needed to give Benkei a rice bowl five times the size of an ordinary man's—he ate so much more than anyone else. Besides, when the family sat down on the floor to have their evening meals Benkei could never sit down gracefully. His arms and legs would never go where he wanted them to. Of course, O'Kin noticed this. Benkei saw her looking at him most unkindly.

One evening after supper Benkei tried to dance. The delicate little paper and wood house trembled. Six of its finest ornaments fell to the floor. Bang! Crash! And five of them were broken. You can be sure O'Kin had plenty to say about that.

"You see how he is," she complained to her father. "And when he tries to use a fan he looks silly. When he tries to bow he looks even worse."

"Have patience," her father said. But again Benkei had heard O'Kin talking.

"I'll show her," Benkei thought.

27

The farmer was doing his best to make Benkei hurry.

Benkei waited until a day when O'Kin was watching while he was unloading rice bags from a cart. The cart belonged to a good-sized farmer who was standing by. The farmer was doing his best to make Benkei hurry the work. "At least I am stronger than anyone else," Benkei thought. He deliberately turned the cart upside down. Then he picked it up by the wheels and shook it vigorously as if it were nothing but a blanket or a piece of silk. "Now it's empty," Benkei said, and walked away leaving the cart standing upside down on the ground.

"Why are you doing that?" screamed the farmer.

"You'll chase away all my trade," said the merchant.

"It isn't my fault," Benkei said. But the merchant knew better.

"What's the use of being strong if you make so much trouble?" he asked.

And again Benkei had no answer.

But the merchant was not a mean man. "Big as you are, you're still young," he said. "I'll have to send you to school. Maybe the priests at the Monastery of the Western Pagoda can teach you better than I can."

"Is the monastery in the mountains?" Benkei asked.

"It is," said the merchant.

"Then I should like to go right away," Benkei announced.

Benkei Goes to School

At the monastery Benkei was taught singing, reading, writing and the True Law of the Lotus. He was a good student and had a fine rich voice.

Benkei's friend Gensakie also came to school at the monastery. Benkei was happy to see him. And for a while things went very well indeed. When Benkei's mother came to visit him, she was most pleased with her son.

One warm summer night the students were having their evening meal in the great hall of the monastery. Benkei had already eaten and did not join them.

Suddenly the students heard a strange noise—grr, grr, grr, grr. It sounded like a large, noisy saw. A few of them decided to find out what it was.

When they followed the noise, they came to the tree where Benkei was lying. He had stretched out fully dressed and had fallen asleep. There he was, snoring loudly.

"Let's play a trick on him," one of them said. "He is so big we could never put anything over on him while he's awake."

So the young student got a paint brush and dipped it in ink. Then he painted "Worthless One" on Benkei's face. He did it so gently with the tip of a camel's hair

30

When they followed the noise, they came to the tree where Benkei was lying.

brush that Benkei did not awaken. Giggling quietly the students tiptoed back to their meal.

When Benkei woke, he again felt hungry. So he walked to the dining hall. Most of the students were still there. When Benkei came in, he was met with loud roars of laughter. Some of the students bent over double, they were laughing so hard. It did not take the Giant long to figure out that everyone was laughing at him. Being laughed at was what Benkei hated most.

Besides, he did not know what the joke was. Then he got a chance to look at himself in a piece of polished metal at the end of the hall. Seeing his painted face, Benkei shook with fury. This was more than he could stand. Still he didn't want the other students to know how angry he was. So although it was late at night, Benkei thrashed off quickly through the wooded mountain paths. Before long he had left the monastery far behind.

The sacred monkeys chattered angrily at him as he woke them in his flight. They did not bother Benkei, who was too angry to care about them. He just kept moving as fast as he could go. Soon he found a little path and followed it.

It led him to a stream that had no bridge. Benkei would not turn back. He took off all his clothes and piled them on his head. Then he waded through the cool water. After washing the ink from his face, he got dressed and tramped on.

At last, however, Benkei grew tired and had to sit down to think. He saw a large fallen tree in the forest and seated himself on it.

"I'll have to show them," he decided. "But how?"

"I know," he said to himself, "I will take them the Bell of Miidera. No one but me could carry it off. When I take it to the Western Pagoda, everyone will remember forever how strong the mighty Benkei is. They will never dare tease me again. And everyone will have to be grateful to me. For the bell is more beautiful than everything in the Western Pagoda."

Then Benkei closed his eyes and tried to imagine how Gensakie and the others would bow in gratitude. He could just hear them telling him what a wonderful gift he had brought them. He could see them whispering among themselves that only Benkei could have gotten it.

By now it was almost morning. So Benkei waited until the next evening, when it again grew dark, and no one could see him. Then he moved carefully through the shadows to where the wonderful bell hung in its belfry.

"Leave me alone, leave me alone," it seemed to say. But Benkei lifted it onto his shoulders and started off. A queer noise in the bushes startled him. For the first time in his life Benkei was really frightened. Was he about to be caught? he wondered. It was too late, he decided, to put the bell back. Instead he hurried away from the sound, toward the monastery.

34

A small rabbit darted out of the bushes. The Giant smiled. "You are what made that noise," he thought.

When he arrived at the monastery, the other students were amazed to see what he was carrying.

"But Benkei," they said, "you shouldn't have done that. You shouldn't have taken the bell. It's not our bell."

Benkei hung the bell up carefully on the monastery ceiling. Then he tried to ring it. The bell would not sound a note. It just whispered to Benkei, "Take me back, take me back."

So Benkei hit it hard with a sword.

The bell just seemed to sigh, "Take me back, take me back." It did not ring. And Benkei grew angry. His gift was spoiled. Now no one would be grateful. He took the sword and struck the bell an awful blow, gashing its side.

"Take me back," whined the bell.

"It's damaged," cried one of the students.

"Why did you bring it here?" asked Gensakie.

"I wanted all of you to be grateful," Benkei admitted.

"You stole it." "You must take it back." "That's no way to use your strength," they shouted, one after another.

"I'm stronger than any of you," Benkei replied.

"We know that," said Gensakie.

"I'm stronger than anyone in the world!" Benkei boasted. "I could stand on the Gojo Bridge and beat any knight that came along and take his sword. I could take a thousand swords from people."

CO. SCHOOLS
6440141

35

"You'd better not try," said the oldest student, "you're in enough trouble now."

"Take the bell back before we are all in trouble," said the youngest student.

Benkei, as usual, was not listening.

"BENKEI!" they all screamed, "Take back the bell!"

Now Benkei had to hear them. But he was more enraged than ever. He yanked the bell from the ceiling and he kicked it all the way back to Miidera.

The monks who owned the bell were very glad to see it. They thought Benkei was kicking the bell because he could not carry it. They had no way of knowing how strong he was. They did not even ask him how he happened to have their treasure.

Although the bell was badly scarred, they thanked him over and over for bringing it back. They even gave Benkei a gallon of soup.

Benkei drank it all down, right away. And then Benkei had an awful feeling. A feeling he had never had before.

Benkei was ashamed. The big Giant felt very small.

When he looked at the deep gash on the wonderful bell he felt even worse.

But he didn't feel bad enough to give up his adventure on the Gojo Bridge.

Benkei was ashamed.
The big Giant felt very small.

At the Bridge

Benkei went down to the city and got himself a new sword. With it he stationed himself on the Gojo Bridge. For several days he terrified the city.

Spreading his feet wide apart, letting his hair fly and

40

waving his sword above his head, he was a dreadful sight. Whenever a group of people who were armed tried to cross the Bridge, Benkei would shout to them.

"Throw down your sword," he called, "or else do battle with me."

Some travelers were much too frightened to fight. They threw down their swords. But then there were others who took up the challenge.

For the next few days, Benkei fought with police, with robbers, with lords and with all comers. He beat them all. At last he had nine hundred and ninety-nine swords. Benkei was almost bursting with pride.

"I'll show them, I'll show them all. I'll have a thousand swords very soon," he murmured.

But no more people came to the Bridge. They were all too frightened. Benkei just waited. He waited in the dark and he waited in the cold.

While Benkei was waiting, a charming young boy dressed in flowing robes of blue silk came along. He was playing a bamboo flute and looked so small and delicate that Benkei had no idea of fighting with him. The boy, however, carried a sword.

"I have been watching you," he said. "You have beaten the robbers, the knights, and even the police. But you can't beat me. My mind and skill are greater than your size. I challenge you to a fight."

Benkei roared with laughter. He roared till his whole

41

big body shook **with merriment**. "Go home, little boy," he said, "you can't fight with me."

The lad had made up his mind to fight with Benkei. Before the Giant knew it, this small stranger had knocked Benkei's sword out of his hand. Benkei quickly grabbed it back and then the fight began.

The boy was so swift and skillful that at first Benkei could not get near him. Sometimes the lad jumped on the rail of the Bridge. Sometimes he darted sideways out of reach. Only once did the swish of Benkei's sword come close to his ear.

Benkei kept tramping back and forth across the Bridge after the little fellow. The boy kept leaping out of the way.

"See, I'm too quick for you," he said. "I'll keep this up till I tire you out and then I'll beat you."

"If I once hit you one of my hard blows," Benkei told him, "that will be the end of you."

He made several quick steps toward the lad. The lad jumped backwards out of reach, lowering his sword as he did so.

"This is my chance," Benkei thought. "His sword is down. He is not protecting himself as he should." The Giant leaped at the boy.

Suddenly the boy's sword was between Benkei's ankles. It tripped the Giant. Benkei fell with a thump, flat on the Gojo Bridge. He had been trapped.

42

Quickly the lad placed his sword over Benkei's head. "Now you can't stand up," he said. And Benkei couldn't.

"Aren't you going to kill me?" Benkei sobbed in terror.

"Not at all. I think you are a very valuable person," said the stranger very gently. "I have never seen anyone **as wonderfully** strong **as** you."

Benkei fell with a thump, flat on the Gojo Bridge.

"What good is my strength?" moaned Benkei.

"All you need is to gain skill and knowledge to go with your strength," the boy replied and put his sword away.

"Who are you?" Benkei wanted to know.

"I am Prince Yoshitsune," came the answer.

Then Benkei jumped to his feet. The young Prince Yoshitsune! He was amazed. And his whole huge body tingled with excitement. "My lord," he said, bowing very low. "My lord, if you will only teach me to be as wise and skillful as you are, I will serve you well with all my strength. I will be loyal to you always, and I will use all my power to protect you from harm."

To this the Prince readily agreed. "I should like that very much," he said, "and I will always be kind to you," he promised.

So the Giant went to serve the Prince as his knight and helper. And Benkei grew in spirit under the kindness of young Yoshitsune. He learned how to use his mind and strength well.

Indeed, Benkei became a wonderful person. He grew to be known as a wise counselor and mighty warrior. And he and young Yoshitsune had many wonderful adventures together.

Their great deeds and brave acts protecting the people of Japan and driving out their country's enemies are praised in song and story to this very day.

44

*"If you will only
teach me to be
as wise and skillful
as you are,
I will serve you well
with all my strength."*